Tiddler's Sewing Box

Shirley Isherwood

Illustrated by Rowan Clifford

To Parents

How to read this book together

- You, as the Storyteller, read the words at the bottom of each page.
- After you have read your part, ask your child to join in with the words in the speech bubbles, and point to the words as they are read.

Remember young children love repetition – it builds their confidence in reading. Always praise good guesses, and if your child is stuck just give the word yourself. This is far more helpful than sounding out individual letters.

The Riddlers of Riddleton End

Talk about the characters your child may have met in **The Riddlers** TV series. There's wise Mossop and his young friend Tiddler, who live at the bottom of the well in Marjorie Daw's garden, and have lots of adventures with Postie the hedgehog and Filbert the squirrel. The books also introduce some new characters – Harvest Mouse, Frog, The Dawn Fairy and a family of mischievous voles.

The Riddlers is a Yorkshire Television Production.

Everything was going wrong
for Tiddler.

First she fell down.
Then she tore her dress.

But worst of all, she couldn't find her sewing box.

Tiddler went to find frog.
"Have you seen my sewing box?"
she asked.

“It has a place for bobbins,
a place for needles,
a place for scissors,
and a special place for the little
silver thimble.”

“Sorry, Tiddler,” said Frog.
“I haven’t seen your sewing box.”

Then he hopped off to have a swim.

Tiddler went to find Harvest Mouse.
"Have you seen my sewing box?"
she asked.

"It has a place for bobbins,
a place for needles,
a place for scissors,
and a special place for the little
silver thimble."

"Sorry, Tiddler," said Harvest Mouse.
"I haven't seen your sewing box."

Then she yawned and went to sleep.

Tiddler went to find Postie.
"Have you seen my sewing box?"
she asked.

"It has a place for bobbins,
a place for needles,
a place for scissors,
and a special place for the little
silver thimble."

“Sorry, Tiddler,” said Postie.
“I haven’t seen your sewing box.”

Then he went on his rounds.

Tiddler began to cry.
"Don't cry, Tiddler," said Mossop.

"We'll wake up early tomorrow and watch out for the Dawn Fairy. She'll bring us good luck."

Early the next morning, the big alarm clock went off and woke up Tiddler and Mossop.

Frog and Harvest Mouse woke up, too.

Tiddler, Mossop, Frog and
Harvest Mouse hid behind the
hedge and waited quietly.

After a while, they saw the
Dawn Fairy shining between the
trees. Then she vanished.

Soon afterwards, over the dewy grass came Vole and her large family.

They were dragging Tiddler's sewing box. All their clothes were newly-patched and the tears sewn up with big stitches.

"We've put everything back!" they said as they ran off.

Tiddler lifted the lid of her
sewing box.

"Everything is in its place," she said happily.
"The bobbins,
the needles,
the scissors,
and **even** the little silver thimble."